Livonia Public Library
ALFRED NOBLE BRANCH
32901 PLYMOUTH ROAD
Livonia, Michigan 48150-1793
(734)421-6600
LIVN #19

JE

8	9	10	11	12	13	14
21	22	23	24	25	26	
33	34	35	36	37	38	
45	46	47	48	49	50	
58	59	60	61	62	63	64
71	72	73	74	75	76	
83	84	85	86	87	88	
95	96	97	98	99	100	

EMILY'S
FIRST 100
DAYS OF SCHOOL

ROSEMARY WELLS

HYPERION PAPERBACKS FOR CHILDREN

NEW YORK

Livonia Public Library
ALFRED NOBLE BRANCH
32901 PLYMOUTH ROAD
Livonia, Michigan 48150-1793
(734)421-6600
LIVN #19

MAY 2 9 2009

With special thanks to JoAnn Jonas, Senior Librarian,
New York Public Library Early Childhood Resource Center

If you purchased this book without a cover, you should be aware that this book is stolen property. It was reported as "unsold and destroyed" to the publisher, and neither the author nor the publisher has received any payment for this "stripped" book.

Copyright © 2000 by Rosemary Wells

All rights reserved.
No part of this book may be reproduced or transmitted in any form or by any means, electronic or mechanical,
including photocopying, recording, or by any information storage and retrieval system,
without written permission from the publisher. For information address
Hyperion Books for Children,
114 Fifth Avenue, New York, NY 10011-5690.

Seventy Six Trombones by Meredith Willson © 1957 (Renewed) Frank Music Corp.
and Meredith Willson Music.
All rights reserved.
Artwork is done in ink and watercolor.
This book is set in 16/26 Kennerley Bold.
Designed by Christine Kettner
Printed in Singapore by Tien Wah Press Pte.Ltd.

Hyperion Paperback edition, 2005
10 9 8 7 6 5 4 3
Library of Congress Cataloging-in-Publication Data
Wells, Rosemary.
Emily's first 100 days of school/Rosemary Wells—1st ed.
p.   cm.
Summary: Starting with number one for the first day of school,
Emily learns the numbers to one hundred in many different ways.
ISBN 0-7868-0507-2 (tr.)—ISBN 0-7868-2443-3 (lib. bdg.)
ISBN 0-7868-1354-7 (pbk.)
[1. First day of school—Fiction. 2. Schools—Fiction.
3. Counting.] I. Title: Emily's first one hundred days of school.
PZ7. W46843Em 2000
[E]—dc21 99-27021

Visit www.hyperionbooksforchildren.com

3 9082 11318 7689

AUTHOR'S NOTE

WHEN I WAS LITTLE, in elementary school, math was no fun for me. It was taught by rote, and it was impossible for me to see how I would use these lessons in real life.

Yet numbers are wonderful things. They appear in all our games, in our poetry, and in songs. Numbers are a vital part of our culture. Some numbers are so much a part of our language that certain things come to mind the moment the number is mentioned; other numbers are shy and need to be brought out of their hiding places. In this book all numbers are equally important, and all are fun.

—*Rosemary Wells*

On the first day of school I leave my mama's arms. I am too excited to cry.

I have my own desk and my own notebook,
and my own teacher, Miss Cribbage.

Miss Cribbage says, "Every morning we will make a new number
friend and write it down in our number books. When we reach one
hundred days we will have a big party." No one believes we will ever
get to one hundred days.

On the second day of school Miss Cribbage teaches us a song
called "Tea for Two." Two is our number friend for the day.
I write it in my journal and on the way home I sing "Tea for Two."

My school bus is the number three bus.
Papa makes sure I know the number three so
that after school I get on the right school bus.

My partner in square dancing is Diane Duck. There are four corners to a dancing square.

After school I pick five different vegetables in our garden. Papa makes tomato-zucchini-pepper-carrot-eggplant soup.

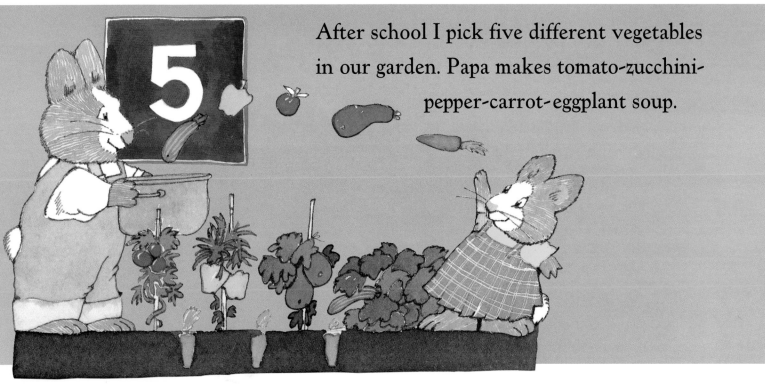

We eat supper at six o'clock. I draw a clock with the little hand at six for my number journal.

he loves me

he loves me not

he loves me

My big sister, Eloise, has a daisy with seven petals. "He loves me, he loves me not, he loves me, he loves me not, he loves me . . ." says Eloise.

"WHO?" I ask. But Eloise won't tell.

My little brother, Leo, has a cold and stays in bed all day. After school I teach him Crazy Eights.

9

Miss Cribbage shows us a map of the night sky.
There are nine planets in our solar system.
I come as Saturn.

Jupiter

Mars

Earth

Venus

Mercury

Saturn

Uranus

Neptune

Pluto

10

Miss Cribbage comes as the sun. "Nine planets plus one sun is ten heavenly bodies," says Miss Cribbage.

11

Every day at quiet time we read a different picture book. We copy the names of the books on paper leaves and pin the leaves to a tree. My book tree has eleven leaves.

12

Leo and I pick Mama a dozen zinnias for her birthday surprise. "Who could have done such a wonderful thing!" Mama says.

Eloise is thirteen years old. She thinks
she knows everything.

Miss Cribbage gives us all gold stars
for writing our names without any
mistakes. I write *Emily* in fourteen
different colors.

My best friend in school is Diane Duck. Her daddy takes us for a boat ride. His motor is fifteen horsepower.
"Is that like fifteen horses swimming?" I ask.

After supper Leo, Eloise, Granny, Grandpa, and I sing "Sixteen Tons."

Miss Cribbage reads aloud
Dick and the Donkey.
I follow along and read
seventeen of the words all
by myself.
"Wow!" says Miss Cribbage.

17

Mrs. Como is blind. Diane Duck and I walk with her across
Main Street. "Eighteen steps from sidewalk
to sidewalk!" says Mrs. Como.
"I know where I am."

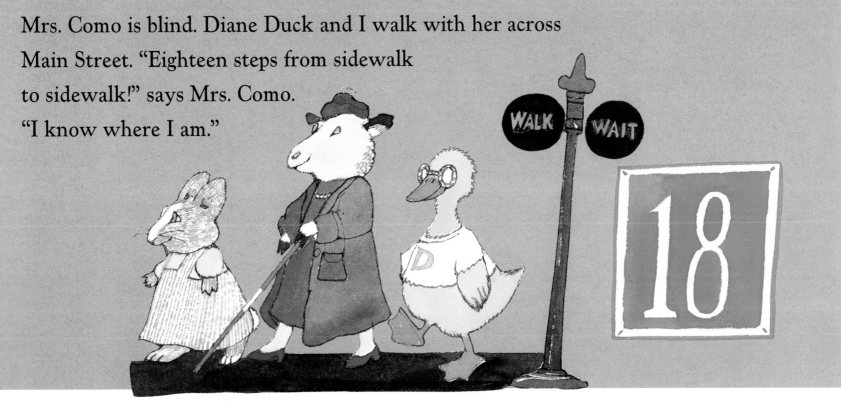

18

Leo eats pineapple upside-down
cake upside down. My mama says,
"You can make pineapple upside-
down cake nineteen ways but only
eat it one way."

19

20

We bring big cardboard cartons in to school.
Miss Cribbage makes three of them into isolation booths.
Then we play Twenty Questions.

ANIMAL

VEGETABLE

MINERAL

21

Today is our music teacher's birthday.
The class sings, "Happy birthday,
Mr. Horne!" and gives him a
twenty-one-horn salute.

Grandpa takes us to a football game.
I count eleven players on each side.
Grandpa helps. Twenty-two footballers
altogether.

Our seats are in
section twenty-three
of the grandstand.

24

Today each family in our class bakes two dozen cookies.
They bring them in for open house night at school.
I draw all twenty-four cookies in my journal.

25

I collect twenty-five Japanese beetles from the garden. I get a penny for each one. Twenty-five pennies make a quarter.

26

There are twenty-six
letters in the alphabet
and I can write them all.
Capital and uncapital.

I read a road sign for our hometown,
North Pleasant Valley by-the-Sea.
That's a twenty-seven-letter name!

27

28

"Don't you want to eat your
vegetable Jell-O?" asks our school lunch monitor.
"I'm counting the peas in it first," I answer.
There are twenty-eight peas in my Jell-O cup.

29

Today a new boy moves to
our school. His name is
Roger and he comes from
Twenty-nine Palms,
California. We look it up
on the map.

30

Miss Cribbage teaches us to recite a poem.

Thirty days has September,
April, June, and November.
All the rest have thirty-one,
Except February, now we're done.

31

32

Eloise has thirty-two Girl Scout merit badges, including First Aid. When Leo falls out of the tree, she makes him a sling from her tie.

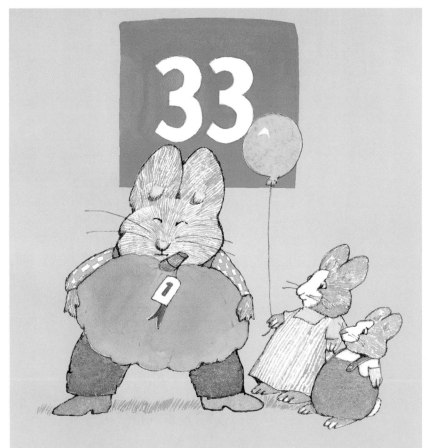

33

The prizewinning pumpkin at the state fair weighs thirty-three pounds.

34

Last night's wind blew acorns onto our front steps. I count thirty-four and make a necklace for Granny.

35

Miss Cribbage has a letter from her brother in Costa Rica. The stamp says thirty-five *centimos*. Someday I'll write a letter all the way to Costa Rica!

Eloise, Leo, and I make growing marks in ink on our kitchen wall. We measure with a yardstick, which is thirty-six inches long.

Eloise shows me the number thirty-seven in her homework. "It's a prime number," says Eloise. "Nothing goes into it. Someday you'll understand." Eloise always says things like that.

38

Our neighbor Mr. Huffington drives a very old car. "It's a thirty-eight DeSoto," says Mr. Huffington. "Best car ever made."

1938

39

"I'm four. How old are you, Aunt Min?" Leo asks. "I am thirty-nine years old," answers Aunt Min. "Still a spring chicken."

40

Papa makes Leo a Noah's ark for his birthday. "The real Noah's ark sailed for forty days and forty nights!" Papa says. After Leo's birthday party Papa takes forty winks on the sofa.

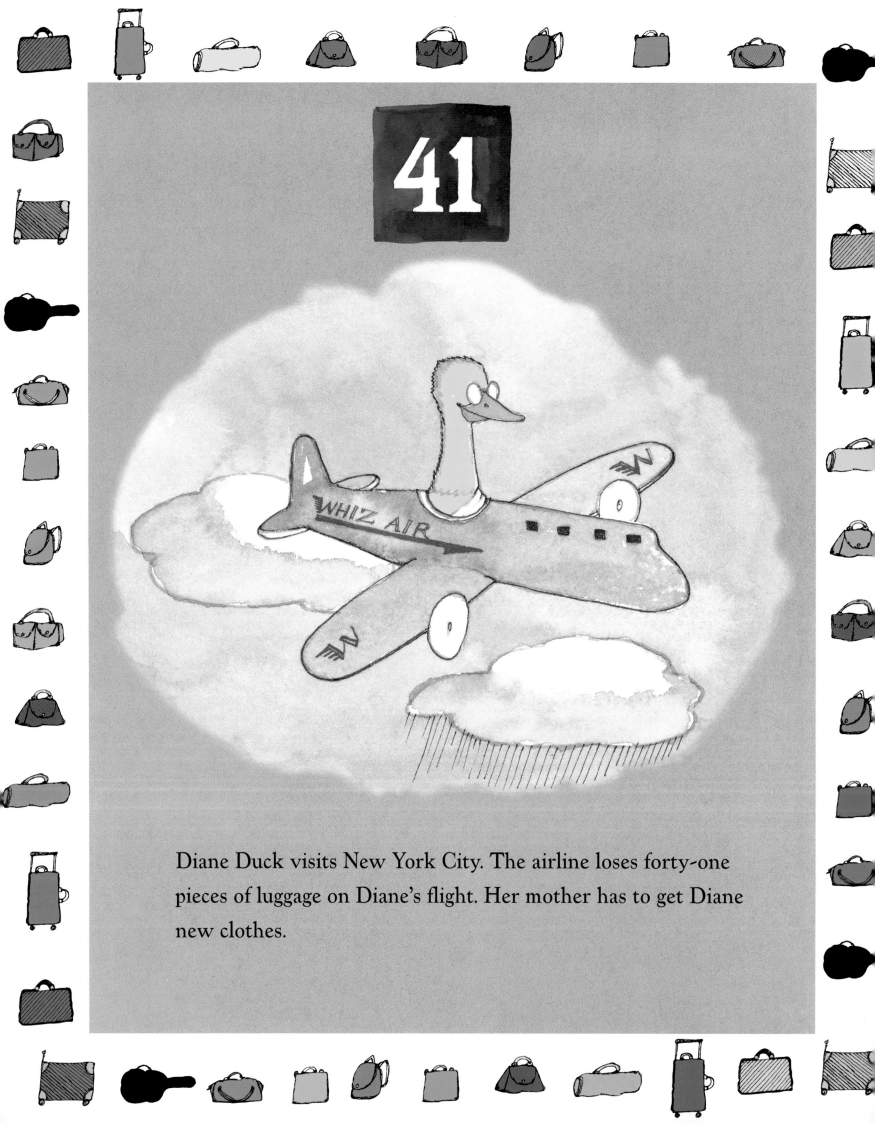

Diane Duck visits New York City. The airline loses forty-one pieces of luggage on Diane's flight. Her mother has to get Diane new clothes.

Diane sends the class a postcard from New York City with a picture of Forty-second Street. I get to read it aloud to the whole class during circle time.

Leo is an astronaut for Halloween. Grandpa makes Leo a space helmet with forty-three fiber-optic meteor-proof antennae on it.

It is Rain Forest Day. Miss Cribbage shows us a picture of
a square foot of Amazon jungle.
"How many beetles can you count?" Miss Cribbage asks.
I count forty-four.

Eloise is learning about triangles. "This one has a forty-five-degree angle on two sides," says Eloise.

The sixth grade boys play the girls in basketball. The score is forty-six to forty-six. Our class are the cheerleaders.

At circle time I read a whole book out loud. It has forty-seven words to it.

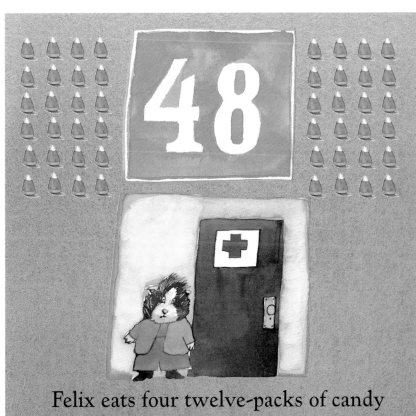

Felix eats four twelve-packs of candy corn from Halloween. The school nurse sends him home with his mama. That's forty-eight candy corns.

49

"Clementine" is my papa's favorite song in the shower. "What's a miner forty-niner?" I ask him. "Someone who went west for gold back in 1849," he tells me.

In a cav-ern, in a can-yon, Ex-ca-va-ting for a mine, Dwelt a

50

Every day we salute our flag. There are fifty stars on it, one for each state. We make a map of the states in our number journals.

51

My sister, Eloise, thinks she is so grown-up, but she is not allowed to go into the big city with her friends. "There are fifty-one reasons why not," says our papa. Eloise does not stay put to hear them.

Because!

52

Diane Duck has moved away, and I am so sad. Granny plays Hearts with me to make me feel better. There are fifty-two cards in the deck, and I know each one.

"Write Diane Duck a long letter with lots of pictures," says my mama. And we do. I make the pictures and Mama writes my words down. We address it to her new house at Fifty-three Buckaroo Boulevard in Pecos, New Mexico.

Diane Duck
53 Buckaroo Blvd.
Pecos
New Mexico

The geese fly over us heading south for the winter. I mark off fifty-four goose dots on Miss Cribbage's nature chart.

	🎃	🍂	🌰	🐦
Emily	·	·	·	·········· ·········· ·········· ·········· ··········
Roger	·	·	·	
Louise	·	·	·	

"Why can't we zoom like the motorcycles?" Leo asks Papa.
"Because the speed limit is fifty-five miles per hour," says my papa.

"How Do I Love Thee? Let Me Count the Ways" is Mama's favorite poem.
"How many ways are there?" I ask.
"Off the top of my head I can count Fifty-six ways," says Mama.

We make piccalilli for class Thanksgiving. The label on our pickle jar says FIFTY-SEVEN VARIETIES on it.

"What are the names of the fifty-seven kinds of pickles?" I ask. But even Miss Cribbage doesn't know.

58

Granny and I take the pies out to cool on Thanksgiving Day. But it is fifty-eight degrees outside. "Indian summer," Granny calls it.

59

At Thanksgiving dinner everyone says thanks for one thing. Leo says thanks for all fifty-nine cranberries in the cranberry sauce.

60

I watch the timer for Mama while she cooks. There are sixty minutes in each hour.

61

Everyone in our class makes
turkey sandwiches for the homeless
people so they have Thanksgiving, too. We make five dozen plus one for Dorothy,
who drives the truck. That's sixty-one sandwiches altogether.

62

Papa and I do the weekly shopping.
There are sixty-two things on Mama's list.

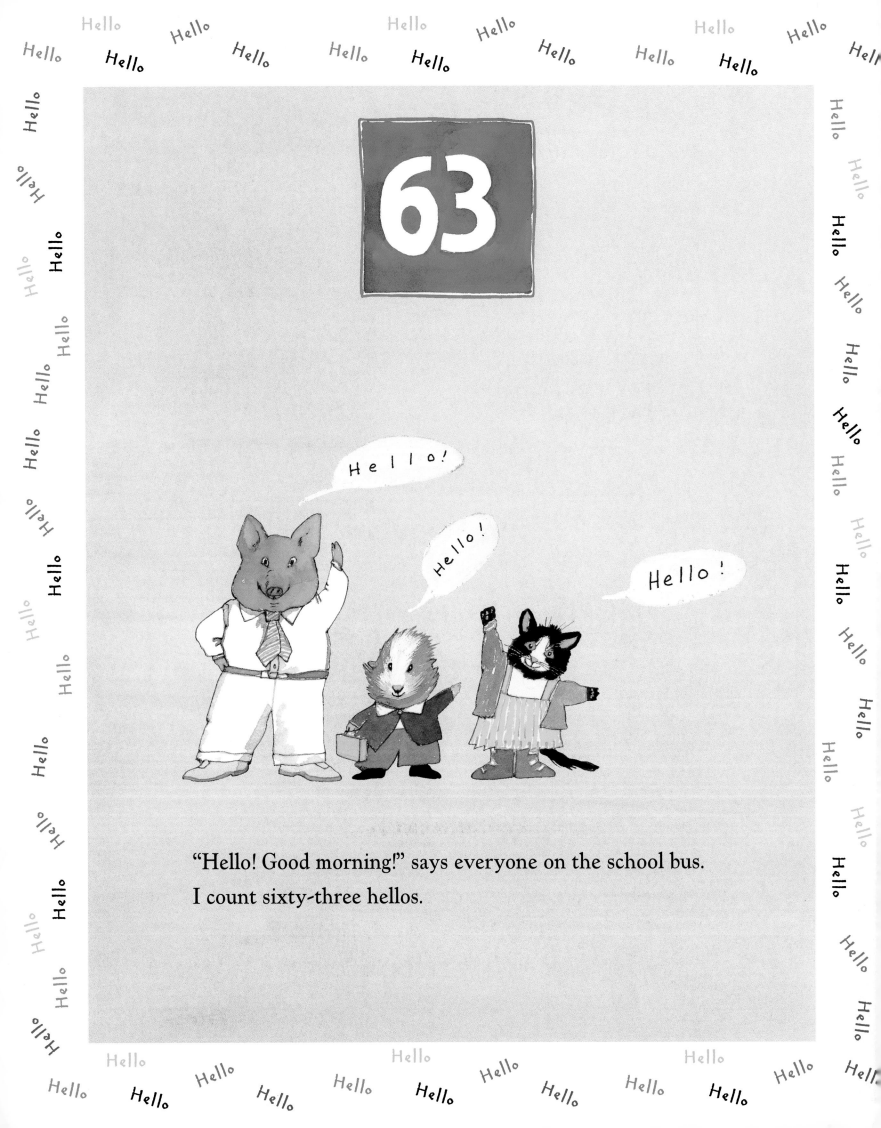

"Hello! Good morning!" says everyone on the school bus.
I count sixty-three hellos.

64

"Why is the sky blue?" Leo asks Granny. "That's the sixty-four-thousand-dollar question," says Granny.

65

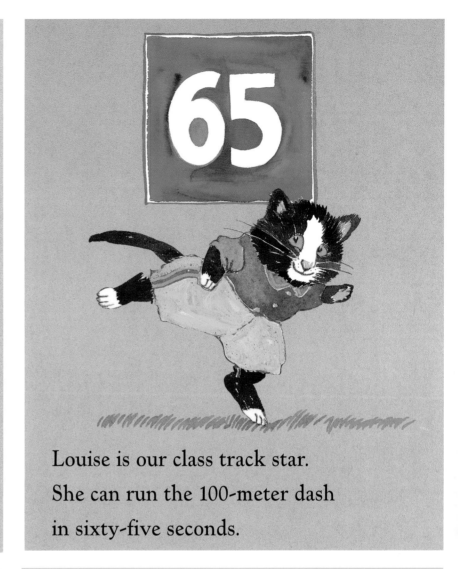

Louise is our class track star. She can run the 100-meter dash in sixty-five seconds.

66

"What will we do when we grow up?" Miss Cribbage asks the class. "I'll drive my very own car all the way along Route Sixty-six right across America. And I'll visit Diane Duck on the way," I answer.

67

Diane Duck sends me mail! It's my first package ever. It has my name and SIXTY-SEVEN OAK STREET right on the envelope. In the package is a tumbleweed.

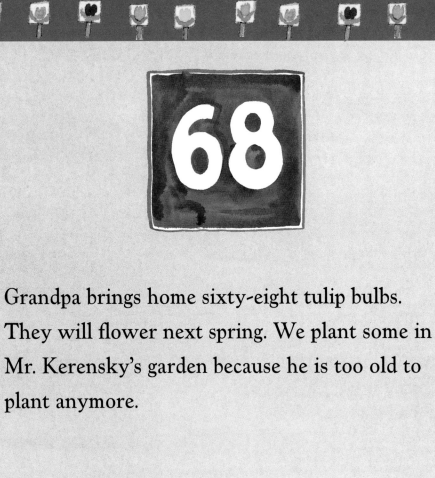

68

Grandpa brings home sixty-eight tulip bulbs.
They will flower next spring. We plant some in
Mr. Kerensky's garden because he is too old to
plant anymore.

69

Eloise plays a duet with Clara for the Girl Scout holiday concert. They have learned "Opus 69" of Beethoven. "That means the sixty-ninth thing Beethoven wrote," says Eloise.

70

Everyone in the lower school lights tiny Hanukkah candles in the cafeteria. Seventy candles make a beautiful sight.

71

Granny and I love to bake. First we measure carefully. "Two scoops of chocolate drops!" says Granny.

"That's seventy-one grams!" I say.

72

Altogether we make six dozen Christmas, Hanukkah, Kwanza, and solstice cookies for the children in the children's hospital.

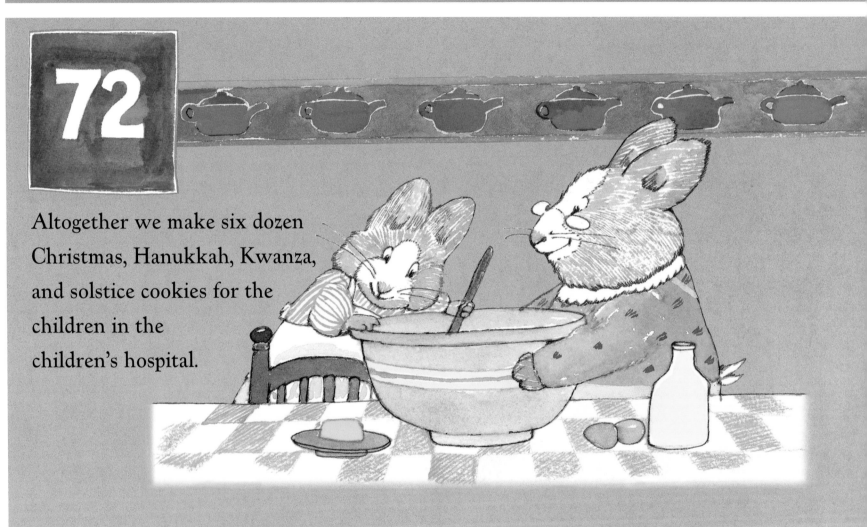

73

Eloise and I make six dozen (plus one for Miss Cribbage's dachshund, Binky) rice-and-egg biscuits for the animal shelter's Christmas dinner.

74

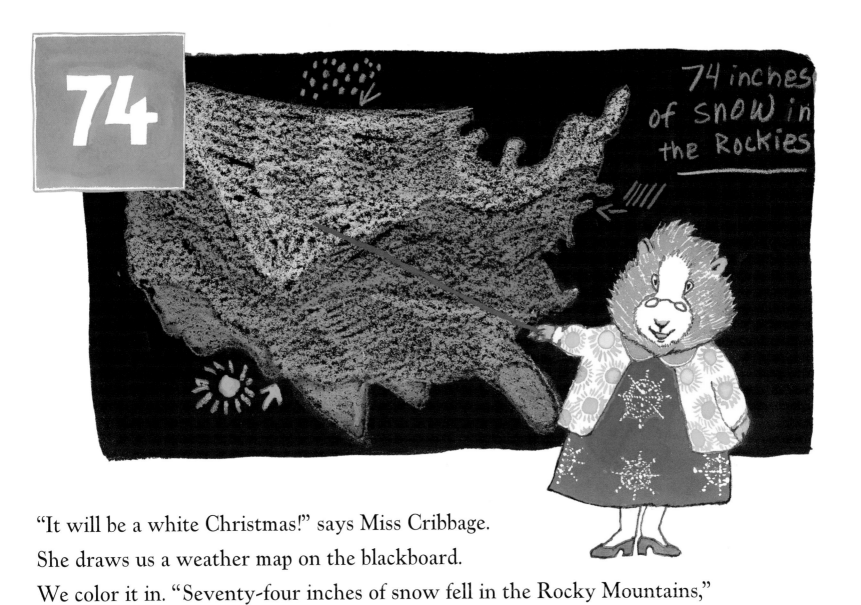

74 inches of snow in the Rockies

"It will be a white Christmas!" says Miss Cribbage.
She draws us a weather map on the blackboard.
We color it in. "Seventy-four inches of snow fell in the Rocky Mountains,"
says Miss Cribbage. "Think of that!"

75

Grandpa is building a clipper ship out of
matchsticks. He keeps a seventy-five-watt
bulb in his work light.

76

Eloise has been asked to play "Seventy-six Trombones" for the Girl Scout jamboree.

"Do you have to practice seventy-six times a day?" asks Papa.

Sev - en - ty Six Trom - bones led the big pa - rade,—

— With a hun-dred and ten cor - nets close at hand.—

Everyone makes a Christmas stocking for the UNICEF Christmas Crusade. Our school sends stockings to seventy-seven children in different countries around the world. I want to write a letter to whoever gets my stocking in a faraway land. I can't write all of the words so I put down:

Happy Happy Happy 🎄!

We string Christmas tree chains. Miss Cribbage dunks them in gold and silver paint. Mine has seventy-eight pieces of silver-painted popcorn.

"What's another word for snowstorm?" asks Mama.

"Blizzard!" I say. Mama shows me how to spell *blizzard* and lets me write it in her crossword puzzle under seventy-nine down.

Angela is a new girl in school. She comes all the way from
Eighty-Mile Beach in Australia.
Angela tells us about Ayers Rock, kangaroos, platypuses
and eucalyptus trees.
Then we find Australia on the map.

81 Miss Cribbage is teaching us about great buildings of the world.
I make an Egyptian pyramid out of eighty-one sugar cubes.
Leo eats the top cube in the car.

82 Angela needs friends. My mama asks Angela's whole family to come for supper. Angela and I skip rope double Dutch eighty-two times without stopping.

83 TROOP 83

Angela's big sister, Freida, is a Girl Guide. Eloise invites her to join Troop 83 of the Girl Scouts of America. Freida says yes and wears her Australian uniform.

84

We make seven dozen cookies for the firemen's ball.
Angela dances to the fireman's fiddle.

85

Our gym teacher does eighty-five jumping jacks every morning.

Our state capitol building is eighty-six steps high to the top of the dome. Our class walks all the way up and all the way down.

86

Angela stays overnight. She is now my best friend. We count
eighty-seven stars in the sky. My mama says Australian stars
are all different, but the moon is the same.

Every Tuesday at lunchtime I sit with Mr. Horne at his piano. There are eighty-eight keys on the piano and Mr. Horne plays them all. I can play and read three notes.

Aunt Min is on a diet. "There are only eighty-nine calories in my tomato soup," says Aunt Min.

"I can't see any," says Leo.

Mr. Goldberg is ninety years old and belongs to the Polar Club. He doesn't mind January ice water and swims every day of the year, winter and summer. "I always have and I always will!" says Mr. Goldberg.

Miss Cribbage tells us her dachshund, Binky, is really an old lady of ninety-one years. (That's thirteen dog years old.)

I turn the radio dial to my favorite station, Country 92, the banjo music station.

93

Angela has never seen ice before, so we take her skating. My papa lets us measure the ice through an ice fisherman's hole. The ice is ninety-three centimeters thick on the pond and that's plenty safe.

A storm knocks down one of our trees. "We'll read the trunk to find out how old the tree was," says my grandpa. There are ninety-four rings in the slice of tree. One for each year.

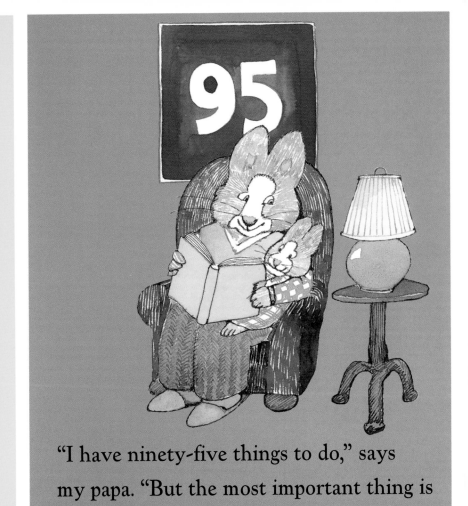

"I have ninety-five things to do," says my papa. "But the most important thing is reading you your story."

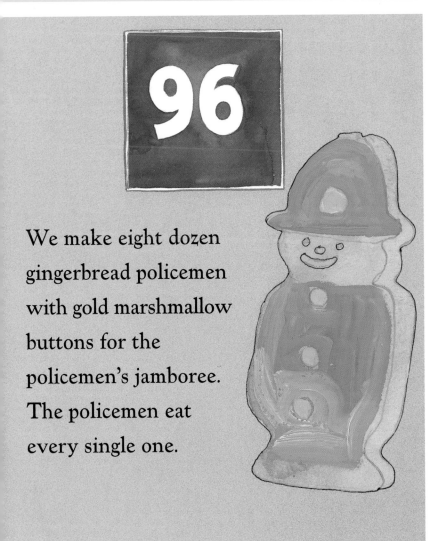

We make eight dozen gingerbread policemen with gold marshmallow buttons for the policemen's jamboree. The policemen eat every single one.

It's Clean Up Our Neighborhood Day! Our class wins the blue ribbon for picking up ninety-seven bottles and cans.

98

I have the sniffles. Mama takes my temperature. "Ninety-eight degrees is normal!" says Mama, but she brings me hot chocolate and lets me stay home from school anyway. In bed I write to Diane Duck. This time my letter is more words than pictures.

99

On my school bus everyone sings. Today we sing "Ninety-nine Bottles of Pop on the Wall."

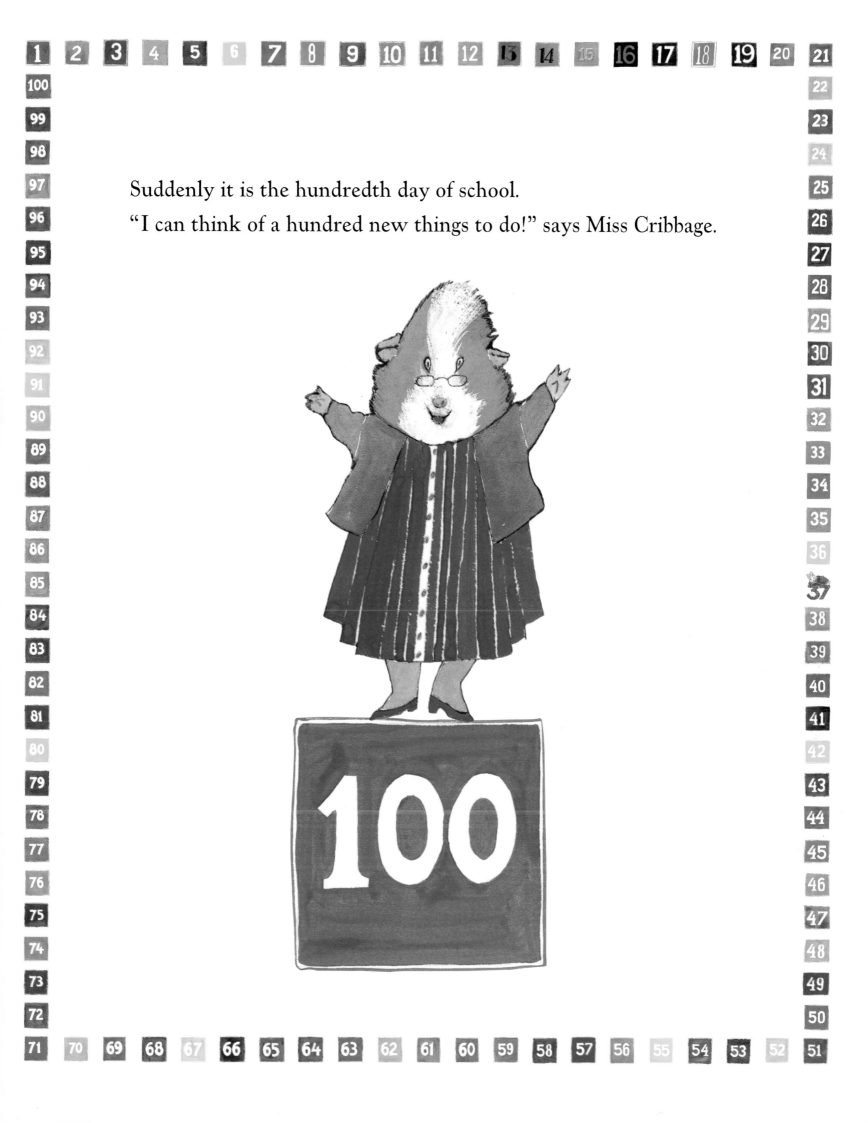

Suddenly it is the hundredth day of school.

"I can think of a hundred new things to do!" says Miss Cribbage.

Felix brings in a
hundred candy corns.

Martha wears a hundred buttons.

Otto plays a hundred
rat-tat-tat-tats.

Roger stands on one foot
for one hundred seconds.

Angela recites a
hundred-word poem.

Terrance does a
hundred cartwheels.

Louise runs a hundred yards.

Lewis makes a glued-together
hundred-bottle-cap hat.

"What are you going to do, Emily?"
asks everyone.
But my hundred is a secret.

8	9	10	11	12	13	14
21	22	23	24	25	26
33	34	35	36	37	38
45	46	47	48	49	50
58	59	60	61	62	63	64
71	72	73	74	75	76
83	84	85	86	87	88
95	96	97	98	99	100